ZENDALA
COLORING BOOK

LYNNE MEDSKER

DOVER PUBLICATIONS, INC.
MINEOLA, NEW YORK

These hypnotic circular images by artist Lynne Medsker offer pages and pages of relaxing coloring. Thirty original designs feature geometric shapes, flowers, and abstract patterns, all radiating from mandala-shaped centers. Colorists with a taste for psychedelic art will particularly appreciate these exuberant illustrations and their intricate details.

Bibliographical Note

Zendala Coloring Book is a new work, first published by
Dover Publications, Inc., in 2015.

International Standard Book Number

ISBN-13: 978-0-486-80251-0
ISBN-10: 0-486-80251-5

Manufactured in the United States by RR Donnelley
80251502   2015
www.doverpublications.com